CHERRY VALLEY DISTRICT L
3 1533 00148 3000
W9-AMB-570

Girls Play to Win

SOCCER

by Jeff Kassouf

Content Consultant
Jack Huckel
Former Director of
Museum and Archives
National Soccer Hall of Fame
and Museum

Norwood House Press
P.O. Box 316598
Chicago, Illinois 60631

For information regarding Norwood House Press, please visit our website at www.norwoodhousepress.com or call 866-565-2900.

Photo Credits: Kirk Strickland/iStockphoto, cover, 10; Felice Calabro'/AP Images, 4; Margaret Pickens/Bigstock, 7; Red Line Editorial, Inc., 8; Andreas Gradin/Bigstock, 14; Gail Newsham/dickkerrladies.com, 16; AP Images, 21; UNC Athletic Communications, 22, 29; Chen Guo/Imaginechina/AP Images, 25, 30; John T. Greilick/AP Images, 32; Luca Bruno/AP Images, 34; Victoria Arocho/AP Images, 37; Michael Caulfield/AP Images, 39; John Todd/AP Images, 40; Kevork Djansezian/AP Images, 43, 47; Roberto Pfeil/AP Images, 48; Lori Shepler/AP Images, 52; Armando Franca/AP Images, 57; Jeff Kassouf, 64 (top); Howard C. Smith/ISIphoto.com, 64 (bottom)

Editor: Chrös McDougall
Series Design: Christa Schneider
Project Management: Red Line Editorial

Library of Congress Cataloging-in-Publication Data

Kassouf, Jeff.
Girls play to win soccer / by Jeff Kassouf.
p. cm. -- (Girls play to win)
Includes bibliographical references and index.
Summary: "Covers the history, rules, fundamentals, and significant personalities of the sport of women's soccer. Topics include: techniques, strategies, competitive events, and equipment. Glossary, Additional Resources, and Index included"--Provided by publisher.
ISBN-13: 978-1-59953-464-0 (library edition : alk. paper)
ISBN-10: 1-59953-464-9 (library edition : alk. paper)
1. Soccer for women--Juvenile literature. 2. Soccer for children--Juvenile literature. I. Title.
GV944.5.K37 2011
796.334082--dc22

2011011037

Manufactured in the United States of America in North Mankato, Minnesota.
177N—072011

Table of Contents

Words in **bold type** are defined in the glossary.

▲ *Teammates celebrate with Alex Morgan (center) after she scored the winning goal against Italy in 2010.*

CHAPTER 1

SOCCER BASICS

With four minutes remaining, the U.S. women's national soccer team needed a goal. The squad was on the road playing Italy. It was the first of two games the teams would play, one in each country. The winner of the series would earn a berth in the 2011 Women's World Cup. But as time wound down in the first game, the score remained tied at zero.

Although men's soccer has enjoyed more popularity around the world than it has in the United States, the opposite has been true in women's soccer. Since the women's game began growing worldwide around the late 1970s, the United States has been a leader on all levels of the sport. Even in 2010, Team USA was ranked number one in the world.

Countries such as Italy were quickly catching up, though. Suddenly, Team USA was in danger of not even qualifying for the Women's World Cup if it lost the series. And then, Alex Morgan stepped onto the field.

The 21-year-old forward had not even graduated yet from the University of California. But she scored what many consider to be one of the most important goals in U.S. women's soccer history. In the 94th minute, during **stoppage time**, Morgan nailed the game-winning goal. When Team USA beat Italy again 1–0 the next week, it was on to Germany for the Women's World Cup. Thanks to young, motivated players such as Morgan, Team USA had lived to play another day.

GETTING STARTED

Soccer is a simple game. It consists of two teams trying to score goals by putting the ball into the other team's goal. When time runs out, the team with the most goals wins. There is one catch, though. Outfield players cannot touch the ball with their hands or arms. Each team has

Soccer Lingo

draw: The result of a game in which both teams have scored the same amount of goals.

friendly: In soccer, an exhibition game.

outfield: The 10 players on a soccer team who are not the goalie.

slide tackle: When a defender slides along the ground, stretching out one foot to knock the ball away from the player dribbling.

one goalkeeper who can use her hands. However, even she can only use her hands while in a certain area, called the **penalty area**.

Soccer teams have 10 outfield players and one goalie on the field. Beginning players might have only five or seven total players on the field, though. No matter how many players are playing for each team, they have to work together to move the ball around the field and to eventually score goals. They move the ball by dribbling, or controlling, and passing.

Soccer played under international rules has a unique game clock. Rather than counting down, the clock counts up. And once it starts, it does not stop again until half time. College and some high school and youth games use a traditional countdown clock like the one used in

▲ *This soccer player races down the field and away from a defender.*

basketball. At the top level, the games are 90 minutes long—or two 45-minute halves. Youth players often play shorter games. There is another catch. The clock does not necessarily stop right when the clock hits 45 minutes. Stoppage time is added to make up for any time wasted by injuries, substitutions, or other breaks in play. It is usually not more than a few minutes per half.

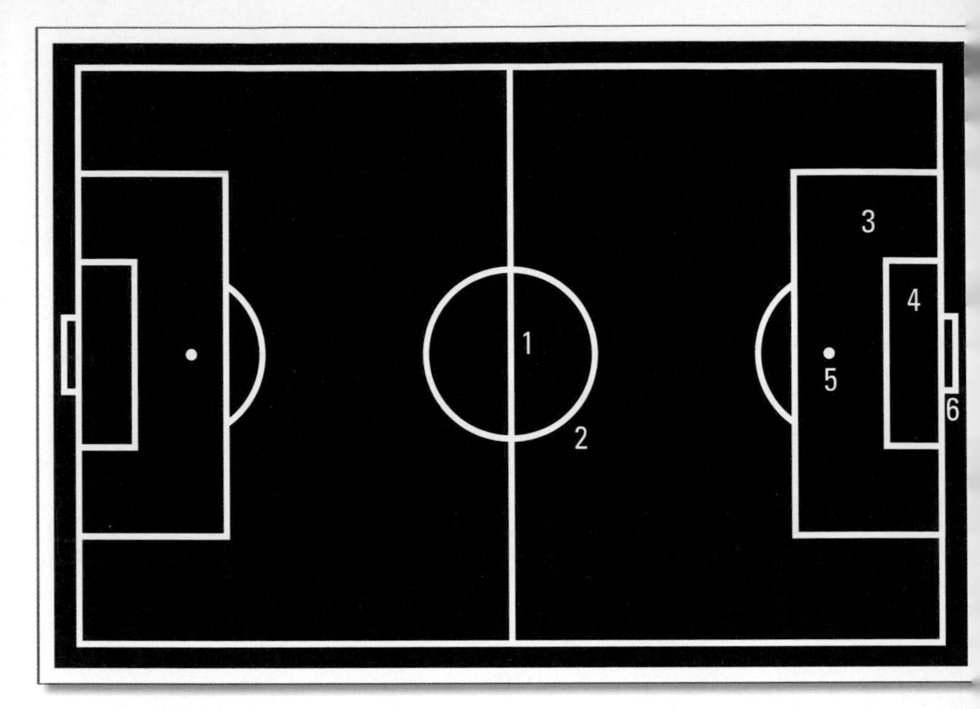

▲ *Soccer field map pointing out halfway line (1), center circle (2), penalty area (3), goal area (4), penalty spot (5), and goal (6).*

THE FIELD

Soccer fields are always rectangular, but they do not all have to be the same size. The maximum size the field can be is 120 yards (109.7 m) long and 80 yards (73.1 m) wide. Sidelines and end lines mark the borders of the field. One goal is in the middle of each end line. There is a **goal area** and a penalty area in front of each goal. When one team sends the ball out of play on the other team's goal line, the defending team restarts play with a goal kick from the goal area. At midfield there is a halfway line with a center circle. This is where the kick-off takes place. Each match begins with a kick-off.

If a foul is committed inside of the penalty area, a penalty kick is awarded to the team whose player was fouled. One player from that team then gets a free shot against the opposing goalkeeper from 12 yards (11 m) away at the penalty spot.

SKILLS

The main objective of soccer is to score goals. Many different moves are required to do that, though. Scoring a goal is often a team effort that requires a series of skills including dribbling, passing, receiving the ball, and shooting. These are all **technical skills**. However, soccer is also a game that requires great **tactics**. The best teams have a strong understanding of both.

Dribbling: When a player is dribbling the ball, she is in control of it. Dribbling involves tapping the ball while

Subs

Throughout a soccer game, a coach can substitute one player for another player. At the youth level, substitutions are usually unlimited. That means that players can be put in and taken out of the game as often as the coach chooses. That's not always the case, though. At higher levels, such as international and professional games, each team is allowed only three substitutions. Once a player is substituted out, she may not reenter the game.

▲ *A player softly traps the ball to take possession of a pass.*

moving around the field. The key is to keep the ball close so that an opponent cannot take it. The best dribblers in the world can move very fast with the ball without ever losing control. By tapping the ball with all parts of the foot, these players can change directions and **juke**, or fake out opponents.

The quickest way to dribble is by pushing the ball forward with the outside of the foot. Once you become a good dribbler, you barely even notice the ball is at your foot. It is just like running.

Passing: Unlike dribbling, passing is usually done with the inside of the foot. Passes can also be made with the outside of the foot and, for the more advanced players, with the head or other body parts. Passing is the quickest way for a team to move the ball around. Passes can help a player get out of trouble if a defender is closing in. They can also be used to set up plays while going for a goal. A player receiving a pass can **trap** the ball in order to stop it. She can also push the ball in another direction under control rather than stopping it.

Shooting: You score goals by shooting. However, goals and shots come in many forms. Some players can score by hitting a hard, driving shot from far away. Other

The Offside Rule

The offside rule is important for keeping order and fairness in a soccer game. The rule says that an attacker cannot go past the next-to last defender if she does not have the ball. The last defender is usually the goalkeeper. So if a team's defenders are stationed around midfield, an opposing forward cannot go behind them and wait for a pass. If she did, she would be "offside." But if she has the ball, or if the ball is kicked to her before she goes offside, she can go past the defenders. The assistant **referee** makes offside calls. He or she stands on the sidelines and looks straight across the field to determine whether or not a player is behind the last defender.

Cards

Serious or reckless fouls could force the referee to give a player a **yellow card** or a **red card**. A yellow card serves as a warning while a red card signals an ejection. An ejected player cannot be replaced. That means her team has to finish the game with fewer players on the field. Two yellow cards given to one player in a game equal a red card. Players can also be suspended for receiving many yellow cards over a series of games.

goals simply require a player to accurately tap the ball toward an open part of the goal.

Most shots are taken with the feet. Powerful shots are usually hit off the top of the foot, where the shoelaces are. Some players try to place or curve shots by striking the ball with the inside of their foot. Some of the hardest shots to take are **volleys**, which are hit while the ball is in midair. A player can also shoot with her head, which is called a **header**.

Tactics: Tactics are all about strategy and mentality. The most basic tactic teams have to choose is which formation they will play in. Formation refers to the number of defenders, midfielders, and forwards a team uses at a given time. The most basic formation is 4–4–2. That means there are four defenders, four midfielders, and two forwards. Formations are always listed in that order. Goalkeepers are not listed because there is always just one goalie. The 3–5–2 formation is another common one. There are only three defenders, five midfielders, and two forwards in that setup.

Formations do not mean players are tied to one area. In fact, it is often hard to identify a formation once the game has begun. As the game develops, players can switch positions or take advantage of open areas on the field.

Formations

Formations dictate how a team plays. The number of defenders, midfielders, and forwards used by each team might seem very simple, but in most cases it is not. For example, while the 4–4–2 formation is the most common, teams play different variations of it. The four midfielders could play "flat." That means they generally position themselves in a straight line across the field. Another option is the "diamond." In that style, the two central midfielders play in front of or behind each other. The midfielder in front is the offensive midfielder; in back is the defensive midfielder. Another common variation is in defense. In a 4–4–2, the four defenders can play flat or with a sweeper and stopper. The sweeper plays behind the rest of the defenders and the stopper plays in front of her.

▲ *Two players battle for control of the ball at midfield.*

SET PLAYS

Some of the most important plays in soccer come while the play is stopped. These are called set plays. They are awarded when the opposing team kicks the ball out of bounds or commits a foul. The team on offense is then able to set up a play.

Corner Kick: When the defending team kicks the ball out of bounds over their own end line, the opposing team restarts play by kicking the ball in from the corner of the field. This can be a great scoring opportunity.

Free Kick: When a player is fouled, her team receives a free kick. Defenders must be at least 10 yards (9.1 m) away from the ball before it is kicked. A direct free kick can be shot on goal. An indirect free kick has to be touched by two players before it goes into the net. Direct free kicks are generally given for more dangerous fouls or fouls such as an illegal slide tackle. Indirect kicks are often awarded for goalkeeper infringements such as holding the ball for too long.

Goal Kick: If the attacking team kicks the ball out of bounds over the opponent's end line, the opponent restarts play by kicking the ball from the edge of the goal area.

Penalty Kick: A direct kick awarded when a player is fouled inside of the penalty area. The penalty kick is taken from the penalty spot, which is centered 12 yards (11 m) from the goal. Aside from the shooter and the opposing goalkeeper, all other players must clear the penalty area.

Throw-In: When one team kicks the ball out of bounds on the sidelines, the other team receives a throw-in. The player throwing the ball in must throw it over her head with two hands and her feet may not leave the ground.

EQUIPMENT

One of the many beauties of soccer is the limited amount of equipment required to play. As a player, all you really need is a uniform, shin guards, and soccer cleats. Official games are played on grass fields, but soccer can be played just about anywhere. As long as you have a ball and some goals, you can play soccer!

▲ *The Dick, Kerr Ladies soccer team from England was at the peak of its popularity around 1921.*

CHAPTER 2

ORIGINS OF THE GAME

Variations of soccer have existed for more than 1,000 years. But the rules of the modern version of the sport we play today were established in 1863 in England. Before then, many English people had played games resembling both soccer and rugby. Very few teams played by the same rules, and the home team often decided which ones to use in each game. In 1863, the two sports split.

Rugby allowed hands, but soccer did not. The Football Association (FA) was created to govern soccer in England. It soon began making formal rules that led to the sport looking like it does today.

Football or Soccer?

Today, most people around the world know soccer as "football." After all, the game is played mostly with the feet. So why do some people—such as Americans and Australians—call the sport soccer? When the FA formed in 1863, it called the sport Association Football. It was often abbreviated as Assoc. Football as opposed to Rugby Football. Rugby players were called "ruggers" so many people began calling Association Football players "soccers" based on the "soc" in the word *association*.

Many new teams formed in England after that. So in 1872, the FA created the FA Cup as the first official soccer competition in the world. The first official soccer league began in 1888 in England. However, those milestones only involved men's soccer.

Women's soccer has been much slower to develop. According to the FA, the first women's soccer match took place in 1895 between the "North" and the "South" of England. The North won the game 7–1. It would be 25 years before the first women's teams from different

Dick, Kerr Ladies FC

Dick, Kerr Ladies FC was the first premier women's soccer team in the world. It was comprised of female factory workers at the Dick, Kerr Co & Ltd. Factory. The team refused to go away even when the FA banned women from playing on official fields in 1921. Instead, the team crossed the Atlantic Ocean in 1922 to play a tour in the United States. With no women's teams there at the time, the Dick, Kerr Ladies FC played nine games against men's teams. They went 3–3–3. That meant they had three wins, three ties, and three losses. Florrie Redford led the team in scoring during the 1922 U.S. tour. Alice Kell was the first captain of the team. Both players were part of the team's first game in 1917.

Women's soccer struggled following the FA ban that limited where they could play. However, the team continued to play matches against the few women's teams that did exist—just not on official FA fields. Dick, Kerr Ladies FC officially disbanded in 1965.

countries met in a soccer game. The Dick, Kerr Ladies Football Club (FC) from England beat a French all-star team 2–0 in front of approximately 25,000 fans.

Dick, Kerr Ladies FC would prove to be superstars of women's soccer during the early 20th century. The club team was based out of Preston, England, and regularly drew big crowds. On December 26, 1920, the team beat St. Helen's Ladies 4–0. An incredible crowd of 53,000 people watched the game at Goodison Park in Liverpool, England.

The team's popularity was taking off, and the future looked bright for women's soccer. But some men viewed the growing popularity as a threat to the men's game. So in 1921 the FA banned the women from playing on Football League fields. That barred women from playing on most English soccer fields. Similar bans in other countries slowed the growth of women's soccer during a time when men's soccer was gaining worldwide popularity.

According to the FA at the time, "The game of football is quite unsuitable for females and ought not be encouraged." And with that, women's soccer in England, the birthplace of the sport, was banned for the next 50 years.

SETTING ROOTS

Soccer was one of many women's sports in which opportunities were limited over the next several years. Many people simply believed women were not supposed to take part in strenuous activities. Those views began to change during the 1970s.

Today, Germany has one of the strongest women's national soccer teams. That country lifted its ban on women's soccer in the fall of 1970. After that, regional leagues began to develop through athletic clubs that already had women's teams in other sports, such as team handball.

In 1971, the English FA ended its ban on women playing on official soccer fields. That same year, the first FA Women's Cup was played. The FA Cup is a tournament in England that includes all club teams, professional or otherwise. A team called Southampton beat a team called Stewarton and Thistle 4–1 in the first FA Women's Cup final.

With the ban lifted, England would again lead the way in international soccer. The England women's national team beat the Scotland women's national team 3–2 in 1972. It was the first official game between two women's national teams.

The first **confederation** to host a women's championship competition was Asia. In 1975, New Zealand defeated Thailand 3–1 in the final of the first Women's Asian Championship. Two years later, Thailand would again lose 3–1. But this time it was host country Taiwan (now referred to as Chinese Taipei) that was victorious. Taiwan won the tournament yet again in 1979, defeating India South. The win established Taiwan as an early force in women's soccer.

SOCCER IN THE UNITED STATES

In the United States, colleges and universities have long played a major role in developing top athletes. Before 1972, however, most of those opportunities were only for men. That changed when the U.S. government passed

▲ *West Germany's Brigitte Klinz grabs Norway's Hege Flognfeldt during the 1981 World Women's Invitational in Chinese Taipei.*

Title IX that year. The biggest change the law made regarded women's athletics. According to Title IX, any program or activity that received federal funding had to give equal opportunities for men and women. That meant, among other things, many schools and colleges had to add women's sports teams. Colleges also had to begin offering **scholarships** for women's sports.

Participation in women's high school and college sports has grown tremendously since Title IX was enacted. The efforts made in the United States and around the world during the 1970s led to a boom in popularity for women's soccer during the 1980s.

▲ *University of North Carolina star Kristine Lilly (right) dribbles away from a defender.*

CHAPTER 3

THE BOOMING '80s

Although Title IX went into effect in 1972, it was not until the 1980s that women's soccer truly began to take off in the United States. A smaller organization held a women's college soccer championship in 1980 and 1981.

But in 1982, the bigger and more established National Collegiate Athletic Association (NCAA) sponsored its first women's soccer championship. Only 12 teams participated in the first tournament. The University of North Carolina Tar Heels defeated the University of Central Florida 2–0 in the final. The Tar Heels had also won the title in 1981. That was the beginning of what would become a **dynasty** for North Carolina.

There were only 77 college teams when the NCAA began sponsoring women's soccer in 1982. By 1990 there were 318 women's soccer teams. College soccer had also expanded into three divisions by that time. The top teams and players were in Division I. Only schools in Division I and II were allowed to offer athletic scholarships. This system remains in place today.

NCAA

The NCAA is the main governing body for college sports in the United States. There are three divisions within the NCAA: Division I, Division II, and Division III. Division I is the highest level of competition. Schools in Divisions I and II are allowed to give athletics scholarships. Within each division there are conferences that teams play in. They help divide teams by region for regular-season competition. Teams then move on to the NCAA championship tournaments, where the national champions are crowned.

Despite the changes, the results did not change much. North Carolina dominated the sport. The Tar Heels won the first three NCAA championships before losing 2–0 to George Mason University from Virginia in the 1985 final. However, North Carolina only became more dominant after that. Beginning in 1986, when college soccer split into multiple divisions, North Carolina won nine Division I championships in a row. The team did not lose a game for eight years.

Years later, it would become clear why those North Carolina teams were so dominant. They featured players who would go on to become some of the best in the world. Among them were high-scoring forward Mia Hamm, speedy midfielder Kristine Lilly, and reliable midfielder Shannon Higgins. During Higgins's four years at North Carolina (1986 to 1989), the team won four championships. Higgins scored the game-winning goal in three of those finals.

THE U.S. NATIONAL TEAM

Just as women's college soccer began to take off in the United States, so did the U.S. women's national team. The United States played its first international game on August 18, 1985. However, it lost 1–0 to Italy in Jesolo, Italy.

The U.S. women eventually became known as the best in the world, but they didn't start out that way. Future

▲ *Michelle Akers (10), shown during the 1991 Women's World Cup, was one of Team USA's first women's soccer stars.*

star Michelle Akers scored the first goal in U.S. women's national team history in a 2–2 **draw** against Denmark. But the team followed that with a 3–1 loss to England and a 1–0 loss to Denmark. The U.S. Soccer Federation fired coach Mike Ryan after those four games in 1985. It hired North Carolina coach Anson Dorrance to replace him. From 1986 to 1994, Dorrance coached both North Carolina and the U.S. national team.

Through 2010, Dorrance remained the only women's soccer coach that North Carolina has ever had. He had become head coach of the Tar Heels before they were even an official NCAA team.

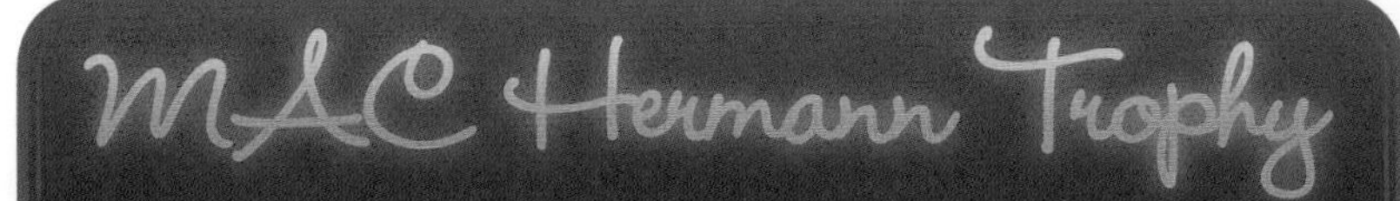

Each year, the Missouri Athletic Club (MAC) hands out the Hermann Trophy to the best male and female NCAA soccer player in the country. It is the most prestigious award a college player can receive. The women's trophy has been handed out since 1988. Some of the earliest winners went on to star for the U.S. women's national team during the 1990s. Among them were: Michelle Akers (1988), Shannon Higgins (1989), Kristine Lilly (1991), Mia Hamm (1992 and 1993), and Shannon MacMillan (1995). The award continued to be a good predictor for international talent. Canada forward Christine Sinclair (2004 and 2005) and U.S. forward Kelley O'Hara (2009) each won the trophy and went on to star for their respective national teams.

When he took over as coach of Team USA, Dorrance began creating a successful program there, too. The U.S. team won five of its seven international games in 1986. Two wins each came against Canada and Brazil while the other was against China. Dorrance won 66 of his 93 games as Team USA's head coach. Many of his North Carolina players starred for his U.S. team as well.

BECOMING A FORCE

China was a heavyweight in women's soccer during the 1980s. Beginning in 1986, it won seven straight Women's Asian Championships. Chinese Taipei from Asia and West Germany, Norway, and Sweden from Europe were also strong teams during the early years of women's soccer. But the U.S. women's national team was quickly catching up.

Team USA began to establish itself as a global power during the late 1980s. Teenagers Hamm (age 15), Lilly (16), and defender Joy Fawcett (19) made their national team debuts on August 3, 1987, in an impressive 2–0 win against China. Brandi Chastain (19) and Julie Foudy (17) made their debuts in 1988. During their many years on the national team together, those players became known as the "Fab Five." Along with Akers and others, they would also become part of what was known as the "Golden Generation" of U.S. women's soccer in the 1990s.

Carin Jennings

Carin Jennings wasn't expecting a tryout for the U.S. women's national team when her University of California, Santa Barbara team played North Carolina in 1987. But with North Carolina coach Anson Dorrance also being the national team coach, that is what happened. And it was a good thing it did. Jennings, now known as Jennings-Gabarra, went on to appear in 117 matches for the United States and earned the Golden Ball as the best player of the 1991 Women's World Cup. She also won the 1996 Olympic gold medal with Team USA and was enshrined in the National Soccer Hall of Fame. Jennings-Gabarra has coached the United States Naval Academy women's soccer team from Maryland since 1993.

The late 1980s saw some ups and downs, though. There were few organized tournaments at the time, so the national team players rarely assembled together. The United States was at even more of a disadvantage than most. Asia, Oceania, and Europe already had continental championships for national teams to play in. Oceania is the area in the South Pacific that includes Australia and New Zealand, among others. With few national women's soccer teams, North America did not have a tournament.

Many of the games Team USA played at the time were **friendly** matches or unofficial tournaments. By 1990, the United States was looking dominant in the games it did play. The team won all six games it played that year while scoring 26 goals and giving up just three. Some of the wins came against good opponents, too.

But to continue that improvement, team officials knew the squad would have to play more games. And to truly test itself against the world's other top national teams, it would need an organized global competition in which to compete. Thanks to the continued growth of the game, both in the United States and around the world, that would soon come. The modern era of women's soccer truly began with the landmark year of 1991.

▲ *Forward Mia Hamm helped North Carolina win four NCAA titles between 1989 and 1993. She made her first national team appearance in 1987 at age 15.*

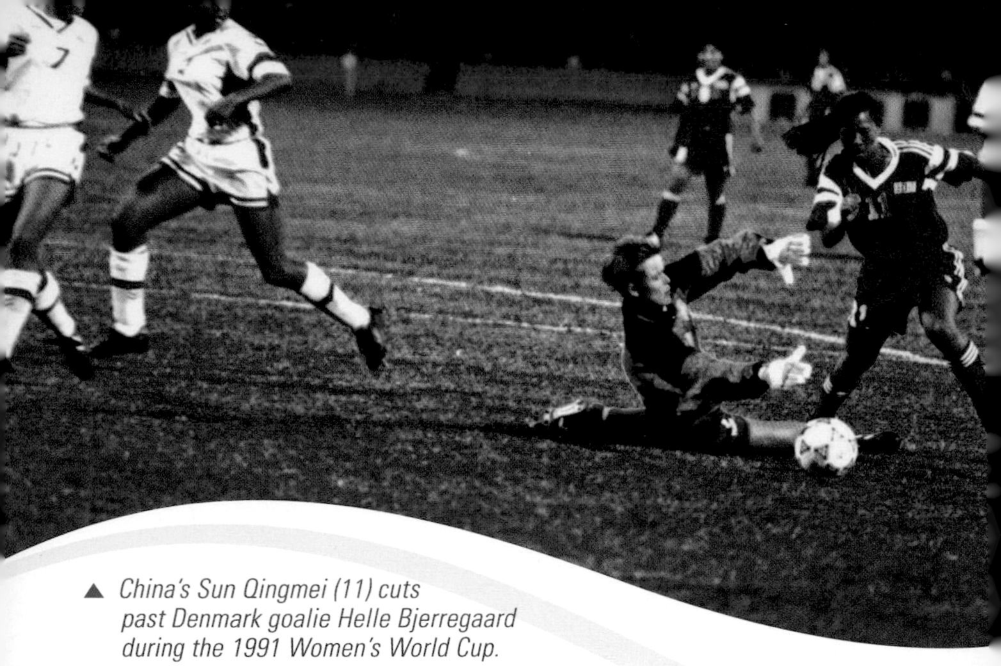

▲ *China's Sun Qingmei (11) cuts past Denmark goalie Helle Bjerregaard during the 1991 Women's World Cup.*

CHAPTER 4

THE WORLD CUP ERA

The Fédération Internationale de Football Association (FIFA) has governed world soccer since 1904. The first FIFA World Cup for men was held in 1930. Sixty-one years later, on November 16, 1991, the first FIFA Women's World Cup kicked off in China. At the time, it was known as the World Championship for Women's Football.

Only 12 national teams competed in the first Women's World Cup. China automatically qualified as hosts. Japan and Chinese Taipei joined out of Asia. Nigeria (Africa), Brazil (South America), New Zealand (Oceania), and the United States (North America) were the lone representatives from their respective confederations. Europe was well represented with five teams: Denmark, Germany, Italy, Norway, and Sweden.

As tournament hosts, China played in the first game. The players delighted 65,000 home fans with a 4–0 win over the favored Norway. Li Ma of China scored the first goal in Women's World Cup history.

International soccer tournaments often have a group stage and a knockout stage. A group stage involves teams being divided into groups, usually of four teams, and playing a round-robin format. The round-robin format means that each team within a group plays each other once. The top teams from each group advance to the knockout stage. This is a single-elimination bracket that determines the champion.

In 1991, China, Norway, Denmark, Team USA, Sweden, Germany, Italy, and Chinese Taipei all advanced to the knockout stage. The United States cruised from there. It beat Chinese Taipei 7–0 in the quarterfinals before beating Germany 5–2 in the semifinals. That set up a showdown with Norway in the final.

Michelle Akers was known for her tremendous work ethic.

MICHELLE AKERS

Michelle Akers is arguably one of the greatest women's soccer players of all time, if not the greatest. FIFA named Akers the women's Co-Player of the Century along with China's Sun Wen. After starring for the University of Central Florida, Akers went on to play 15 years for the U.S. national team beginning in 1985. She scored 105 goals and added 37 assists in the process.

Akers, however, was known more for her work ethic than her statistics. She frequently played until she was so exhausted that she collapsed. Later in her career, she was diagnosed with chronic fatigue syndrome. In the 1999 Women's World Cup semifinal against Brazil, Akers played herself to such exhaustion that her jersey had to be cut off with scissors on the sideline. Still, she marched on as the heart and soul of the U.S. team for three Women's World Cups. "She is our everything," Mia Hamm once said about Akers.

U.S. forward Michelle Akers had been a breakout star throughout the tournament. Her abilities continued to shine bright in the final. Her goals in the 20th and 78th minutes gave the United States the first Women's World Cup title. Shannon Higgins assisted both goals. Akers ended the tournament with 10 goals in six games. For her efforts, she won the Golden Shoe as the tournament's top goal scorer.

Akers's teammate, Carin Jennings, scored six goals throughout the Women's World Cup. She was awarded the Golden Ball as the tournament's best player. The tournament even provided an opportunity for Brazilian referee Claudia de Vasconcelos to become the first woman to officiate at the World Cup level. She refereed the third-place match between Germany and Sweden.

Although the Women's World Cup was much smaller than it is today, the first tournament did offer a glimpse into the future. The teams that would dominate the sport for the next two decades all qualified for the tournament. Brazil, Germany, Nigeria, Norway, Sweden, Japan, and the United States—more than half of the 1991 participants—have qualified for every Women's World Cup through 2011. China missed the tournament for the first time in 2011.

MORE GROWTH

Like the men's World Cup, the Women's World Cup takes place every four years. Team USA came into the

▲ *U.S. star Shannon MacMillan scores against China during the gold medal game at the 1996 Olympic Games.*

1995 edition in Sweden as favorites to repeat. However, an injury to Akers in the first game made things harder. Without the star forward, the United States' hopes of a second consecutive title ended in the semifinals. Norway, defending its loss from the 1991 tournament, beat Team USA 1–0. Ann Kristin Aarønes scored the only goal in the 10th minute.

Team USA ended up finishing third. Meanwhile, Norway went on to defeat Germany 2–0 in the final. Aarønes scored six goals throughout the tournament and won the Golden Shoe. Her teammate, Hege Riise, won the Golden Ball. Like Team USA, Norway had clearly established itself as one of the early powers in the Women's World Cup era.

THE OLYMPIC GAMES BEGIN

Women's soccer took another major step forward the next year when it debuted in the 1996 Olympic Games. There was not enough time to hold a qualifying tournament, so the eight best teams from the 1995 Women's World Cup showed up in Atlanta, Georgia, for the Games. Among them were powerhouses Team USA, Norway, Sweden, China, and Germany.

The developing rivalry between Team USA and Norway had another chapter in the Olympic semifinals. This time, the United States was victorious with a 2–1 overtime win. That set up a USA-China final.

The gold-medal game was a preview of the magic that would come three years later. A total of 76,489 fans came to Sanford Stadium in Athens, Georgia, for the game. They were in for a treat. Shannon MacMillan, who quickly became known for her hard shots, gave the United States

Inspiration

"I grew up looking up to them," said Jessica Mendoza, who later became a U.S. Olympic softball player, about the U.S. women's soccer team. "They were the first team that paved the way for women's sports in our country. After that first gold medal in 1996, a lot of girls felt like they could play sports."

Sun Wen

Along with Michelle Akers, China forward Sun Wen was also named the FIFA Co-Player of the Century. Wen scored more than 100 goals for China, and she was instrumental in leading the team to the 1999 Women's World Cup final. She won the Golden Ball Award as the 1999 Women's World Cup top player and the Golden Shoe Award for being the top goal scorer. Sun Wen was the most feared attacker by U.S. defenders, and although the USA-China rivalry was fierce, there was a lot of respect for each other. "Akers was their key player," Sun said after the final. "If not for her, we would have been more successful getting forward." If not for Sun, China would have had far less success scoring goals and advancing to the final.

the lead in the 19th minute. But China's Sun Wen tied it 12 minutes later. The deadlock remained until the 68th minute. Then, U.S. forward Tiffeny Milbrett broke the tie. Her shot ended up being the game-winning goal. The United States beat China 2–1.

AN AMAZING SUMMER

All of the momentum from the first two Women's World Cups and the 1996 Olympic Games led to an exciting 1999 Women's World Cup. Many credit the success to the popular U.S. women's national team. People loved that they seemed so personal and fun, but that they also won. The U.S. players were nicknamed "The Girls of Summer" because of all the attention they got that summer.

▲ *Team USA star Mia Hamm signs autographs for young fans after a practice at the 1999 Women's World Cup. Hamm and her U.S. teammates caught the nation's attention that summer.*

It became clear that the 1999 Cup was going to be a big deal from the opening game. Almost 79,000 fans showed up at Giants Stadium in New Jersey to watch Team USA beat Denmark 3–0. The star trio of Mia Hamm, Julie Foudy, and Kristine Lilly each scored a goal that game. The excitement only grew from there.

More than 50,000 fans showed up for Team USA's third game, which was held outside Boston, Massachusetts. The U.S. team delighted fans with a 3–0 win over North Korea. Fans took notice of other teams as well. Brazil and Germany were emerging as two of the best teams in the world. Their 3–3 draw in the group stage attracted 22,109 fans to the Washington D.C. area.

The 1999 tournament was the first Women's World Cup to feature 16 teams. In total, more than 650,000 fans filled the stadiums for the 32 Cup games that summer. Even the media coverage was expansive. In the United States alone, approximately 40 million watched on TV. Nearly 2,500 journalists covered the event. For the first time in its history, the Women's World Cup was treated as a truly major event.

RUN TO THE CUP

As Team USA continued to win, fan interest grew across the country. In the semifinals, the United States beat Brazil 2–0 and China beat Norway 5–0. That set up an anticipated rematch of the 1996 Olympic gold-medal game in the finals.

Sun entered the final as the tournament's standout player. She had already scored seven goals in the tournament. Only Brazil's Sissi had scored that many. Team USA, meanwhile, got to the final by focusing on defense and teamwork. Milbrett led the team in scoring with just three goals in the tournament. Five of her teammates scored two goals apiece. A crowd of 90,185 fans showed up at the Rose Bowl in Southern California for the game. No women's sporting event has ever drawn more fans.

For the 1999 Women's World Cup, Akers moved from forward to the defensive midfield role. She anchored the team and played a key role in slowing down the Chinese offense. After 90 minutes of back-and-forth play, the teams were tied 0–0. They remained tied after 30 minutes of **extra time** as well. That led to a **penalty shootout**.

The first four U.S. shooters all made their shots. U.S. goalie Briana Scurry, however, saved China's third shot. So when U.S. defender Brandi Chastain stepped forward to take the fifth shot, the game was in her hands.

She approached the ball and struck it with her left foot. When the ball crashed into the inside right netting of the goal, Team USA had secured the victory. In a moment of joy, Chastain ripped off her jersey and dropped to her knees screaming. She had just scored perhaps the most famous goal in the history of women's soccer.

Brandi Chastain celebrates at the 1999 Women's World Cup championship.

BRANDI CHASTAIN

Brandi Chastain played a major role for Team USA at the 1999 Women's World Cup, but she was hardly the face of the team. She originally joined the team as a forward, but was cut after the 1991 Cup. After rejoining the team a few years later, Chastain established herself at left back. Then, on July 10, 1999, she scored the winning goal in the Women's World Cup. An image of Chastain celebrating graced the cover of Sports Illustrated, Newsweek, *and* TIME *magazines, among others. The images of Chastain's celebration were empowering to many women.*

▲ *Brazil and San Jose CyberRays star Sissi celebrates after scoring during a 2003 WUSA game.*

CHAPTER 5
THE PROFESSIONAL ERA

The 1999 Women's World Cup was so successful that organizers had an idea that would have been unthinkable just a decade before: a women's professional soccer league in the United States. Behind millionaire John Hendricks, the Women's United Soccer Association (WUSA) was formed in 2001.

The creation of WUSA was a momentous achievement for women's soccer. The league gave the top women's soccer players an opportunity to play outside of their national teams. While players had to be citizens of a country to play on its national team, players of any nationality could play in WUSA and other professional leagues. And while other women's soccer leagues existed in Europe at the time, WUSA became the first women's soccer league in the world to pay every player. That immediately made it the world's premier women's soccer league.

Many of the stars from the 1999 Women's World Cup were featured on the eight WUSA teams. They included China's Sun Wen, Germany's Birgit Prinz, Brazil's Sissi, and all of the U.S. women's national team members. The WUSA teams were spread all across the United States.

WUSA got off to a strong start in 2001. The women played attractive, offensive soccer, and games averaged 8,116 fans. U.S. star Tiffeny Milbrett, playing for the New York Power, was the league's Most Valuable Player (MVP) that year. She scored 16 goals and added three assists.

The WUSA championship game was called the Founders Cup. The Bay Area CyberRays of California defeated the Atlanta Beat in a penalty shootout to win the 2001 Founders Cup.

On the field, the league was a success. It gave fans a way to regularly see their favorite players, such as U.S.

Marinette Pichon

Forward Marinette Pichon of France played in the WUSA for the Philadelphia Charge. She won the 2002 MVP Award while leading the Charge to the league semifinals. "This is a great honor because the players in the WUSA are the best in the world," Pichon said. She scored 14 goals that season. Pichon did not have as much success playing with France. Her lone Women's World Cup experience was in 2003. Although Pichon scored two goals, France went 1–1–1 and failed to advance out of the group stage.

stars Mia Hamm, Brandi Chastain, and Julie Foudy. It also gave an opportunity for young players to develop into stars. Among them were England's Kelly Smith, Germany's Maren Meinert, Canada's Charmaine Hooper, Scotland's Julie Fleeting, and France's Marinette Pichon.

Off the field, however, the league struggled to make money. WUSA folded following the 2003 season. It was just days before the beginning of the 2003 Women's World Cup kicked off. The dream of a professional women's soccer league would have to wait.

REBUILDING

The 2003 Women's World Cup was set to take place in China. However, due to an outbreak of the SARS virus it was moved to the United States. With less time to

U.S. forward Mia Hamm dribbles around a Brazil defender during the gold-medal game at the 2004 Olympic Games.

MIA HAMM

*During her long career, Mia Hamm became the first superstar of women's soccer. She joined the U.S. national team in 1987 and played until 2004. During that time she won two Women's World Cups and two Olympic gold medals. She retired as the world's all-time leader for goals scored (158), assists (144), and **points** (460). Hamm also has the most **hat tricks** (10) in U.S. history. Hamm won the first-ever FIFA Women's World Player of the Year Awards in 2001 and 2002.*

But statistics do not describe Hamm's overall impact. She was a smiling, friendly face that people could identify with. Yet she was also an ace on the soccer field. Her talent and charisma made her the first—and perhaps only—U.S. soccer player to gain mainstream commercial appeal and popularity. Hamm is so iconic to women's soccer that the Women's Professional Soccer logo features a shadow of her as the main graphic.

prepare and the Golden Generation of U.S. players getting older, excitement for the 2003 Cup did not live up to that surrounding the 1999 Cup.

The stadiums were smaller, and fewer fans came to the games. Media coverage was not what it had been, either. Part of that might have been because Team USA did not fare as well as it had in 1999. Still, a mix of older players such as Hamm and Foudy and younger players such as forward Abby Wambach and midfielder Shannon Boxx led the United States to a third-place finish.

The bigger story from the 2003 World Cup was the emergence of more strong teams, especially those from Europe. For more than a century Europe has been at the center of men's soccer. The women were rapidly catching up. Four of the final eight teams were from Europe. None was more impressive than Germany. Behind Nia Kuenzer's extra-time goal, Germany beat Sweden 2–1 in an all-European final.

With no professional women's soccer league in the United States, many top female players had to find a new way to play between national team competitions. Some decided to play in the U.S.-based W-League. However, that league could not offer pay to all of its players. Others played with professional teams in Europe. For many of the top U.S. women, they trained year-round with the national team.

Fall of Powers

As new international soccer powers emerged during the 2003 Women's World Cup and the 2004 Olympic Games, the countries that had dominated the sport previously began to fall. Team USA survived the transition. China and Norway did not fare as well. China had finished second during the 1996 Olympic Games and the 1999 Women's World Cup. However, the upstart Canadians beat China 1–0 in the 2003 quarterfinals. Norway, which had won the 2000 Olympic Games, lost 4–1 to Brazil in the group stage before losing to Team USA in the quarterfinals. In 2004, China lost a group-stage game 8–0 to Germany and tied Mexico en route to a first-round elimination. Norway, meanwhile, failed to even qualify for the 2004 Games.

A LAST HURRAH

The Olympic Games are the second biggest competition in women's soccer, behind the Women's World Cup. After sliding to third place at the 2003 Cup, the U.S. players were determined to win the 2004 Olympic Games in Athens, Greece. They had extra motivation: The 2004 Games would be the last major international tournament that the "Fab Five" would play in together. Although Chastain and Kristine Lilly continued their national team careers, U.S. legends Hamm, Foudy, and Joy Fawcett had announced they would retire afterward.

It was not an easy task. As the United States had learned in 2003, the number of countries with strong national teams had grown greatly since the first Women's World Cup in 1991. Brazil, the all-time most successful country in men's soccer, was establishing itself as a power in women's soccer. Already established countries such as Germany and Sweden continued to improve as well. Even emerging countries such as Australia, Japan, Mexico, and Nigeria were becoming formidable opponents in the early rounds.

Germany surprised many by eliminating the powerful U.S. team in the semifinals of the 2003 Women's World Cup. The Germans had a chance to do it again in the 2004 Olympic semifinals. They almost did it, too. Lilly put Team USA up 1–0 in the 33rd minute. But Germany's Isabell Bachor tied the game in stoppage time. It took an extra-time goal from U.S. midfielder Heather O'Reilly to get the U.S. squad back to the final.

Another strong opponent waited. The young but talented Brazil squad had dazzled fans with its offensive play throughout the tournament. Behind exciting 18-year-old forward Marta Vieira da Silva—known simply as Marta—Brazil appeared ready to challenge the experienced United States. And they did indeed challenge the Americans.

It was a tight game from the start. Lindsay Tarpley gave Team USA the lead in the 39th minute. Then Brazil came back when Pretinha scored the tying goal in the 73rd. Both sides turned up the intensity, desperately trying to

▲ *U.S. stars (from left) Julie Foudy, Joy Fawcett, Mia Hamm, Kristine Lilly, and Brandi Chastain celebrate after winning their last major championship together at the 2004 Olympic Games.*

notch the winning goal in regular time. But neither was successful. So for the second game in a row, Team USA went into extra time. The excitement continued until the 112th minute. That is when Wambach headed in the goal that ended the Fab Five era with an Olympic gold medal.

"We wanted to send them out on top," Tarpley said, referring to Hamm, Foudy, and Fawcett. "They've done so much for the women's game. To be able to win gold when some of them are retiring—it's a great night."

It was a night of transition as well. As Hamm, Foudy, and Fawcett competed in their last major game, the 24-year-old Wambach cemented her place as the next U.S. star. However, Wambach and the next generation of U.S. players would have to compete with a new bona fide power in Marta and Brazil.

▲ *Germany's Birgit Prinz (left) was the FIFA World Player of the Year in 2003, 2004, and 2005.*

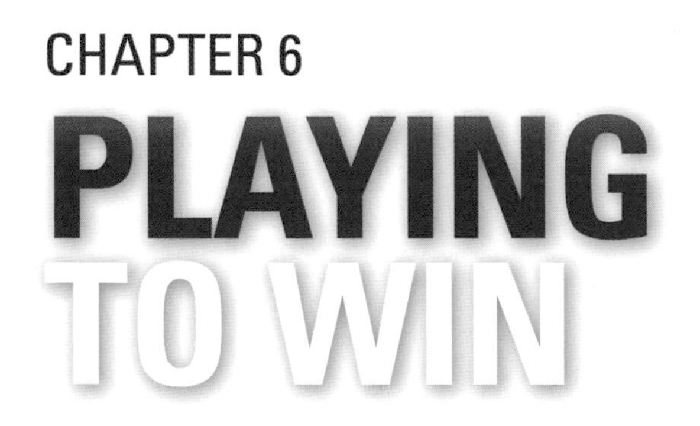

CHAPTER 6
PLAYING TO WIN

For years, U.S. players such as Mia Hamm and Julie Foudy had dominated the international soccer landscape. A new generation of women's players, both in the United States and around the world, truly emerged following the 2004 Olympic Games.

Behind star forward Birgit Prinz, Germany continued to cement itself as a women's soccer power with a win in the 2005 Women's European Championship. As in men's soccer, many other strong teams came from Europe. However, as the women's game grew in popularity and more women got opportunities to play, women's soccer was rapidly growing around the world.

In Africa, Nigeria continued to establish itself as a power by winning the 2006 African championship. China also rebounded from some rough times to win the 2006 Asian championship. In South America, Brazil had become one of the world's best teams. But even it was not unbeatable. Argentina shocked Brazil in 2006 to become the South American champions for the first time.

Birgit Prinz

Many people consider Germany forward Birgit Prinz to be the best women's soccer player of her time. It's hard to argue against it. Prinz has scored 14 goals while playing in 22 Women's World Cup matches (1995, 1999, 2003, and 2007). She was named FIFA World Player of the Year in 2003, 2004, and 2005. Prinz played for FFC Frankfurt in Germany for most of her professional career, although she did play for the Carolina Courage of the WUSA in 2002 and 2003. Prinz helped Carolina win a championship in 2002, scoring 12 goals that year.

The 2007 Women's World Cup, however, was all about Germany and Brazil. The defensive-minded Germans had not allowed a single goal leading up to the final. The free-flowing Brazilians, however, had already scored 17 goals in their five Women's World Cup games. Four of them came in a 4–0 drubbing of Team USA in the semifinals.

Marta and Brazil put up a strong effort, but it was not enough to get past Germany. Prinz put her team up in the 52nd minute and Simone Laudehr secured the 2–0 victory with a goal in the 86th. Germany goalkeeper Nadine Angerer might have been the biggest star, though. She saved a Marta penalty kick that would have tied the game. Her 517 minutes of Women's World Cup play without giving up a goal—including all six of the games in 2007—was a new record. It helped Germany become the first country to ever repeat as Women's World Cup champions.

A NEW OPPORTUNITY

After finishing third at the 2007 Women's World Cup, the United States achieved more major milestones in 2008 and 2009.

Behind stars such as goalie Hope Solo, midfielder Heather O'Reilly, and forward Amy Rodriguez, Team USA won a gold medal at the 2008 Olympic Games in Beijing, China. U.S. midfielder Carli Lloyd scored in extra time to give the United States a 1–0 victory over Marta and Brazil.

Less than a year later, in 2009, Women's Professional Soccer (WPS) debuted in the United States. After the disappointing end to WUSA, WPS's backers were determined to create a sustainable professional women's soccer league in the United States. Like the WUSA, the WPS quickly became known as the premier women's soccer league in the world.

Rodriguez, who was still in college during the Olympic Games, was the first player selected in the WPS draft. Several other stars—both from the United States and around the world—also came to the league. It began with seven teams spread around the United States.

International Leagues

In the absence of the WUSA, other professional leagues around the world grew. One was the Frauen Bundesliga in Germany. It began its modern era in 1997 and quickly became one of the best leagues in the world. Top German players such as Birgit Prinz and Inka Grings played there. Other top European leagues include Damallsvenskan (Sweden), Toppserien (Norway), and the FA Women's Super League in England. The Women's Super League began in 2011 with eight teams. Some of those teams had previously played in the FA Women's Premier League, which is now England's second division. Since WPS debuted in 2009, many people have considered it to be the top women's league in the world.

▲ *Brazil star Marta (right), playing for the Los Angeles Sol, dribbles away from Francielle (24) and Christie Rampone (3) of Sky Blue FC during the 2009 WPS title game.*

MARTA

WPS got off to a good start as a league when it convinced the best player in the world to join. Brazilian forward Marta won five straight FIFA Women's World Player of the Year Awards from 2006 to 2010. Many consider her to be the most entertaining women's player of all time. Her crafty dribbling skills, speed, and ability to score goals have brought her the unprecedented honors.

Marta first made a name for herself with Brazil. She caught the world's attention as a teenager by displaying tremendous flair at the 2003 Women's World Cup and 2004 Olympic Games. Through 2010, she has led Brazil to the championship in two Olympic Games and one Women's World Cup. But she is still searching for her—and Brazil's—first championship in those tournaments.

Marta's WPS career has spanned three different teams in the league's first three seasons. As the league MVP, she led the Los Angeles Sol to the 2009 title game. She was the league MVP again in 2010. This time she led her team, FC Gold Pride, to the WPS championship. Before the 2011 season, Marta joined the Western New York Flash.

The moves meant more fans were able to cheer for Marta on their home team. However, they were made out of necessity. The young league struggled in some areas. Each of Marta's first two teams ran out of money and had to fold. WPS entered the 2011 season with six teams, but only three remained from the league's inaugural 2009 season.

EUROPEAN STARS

Germany has had one of the top women's national teams since the Women's World Cup debuted in 1991. The country continues to produce some of the top players in the world. Forwards Prinz and Inka Grings helped lead Germany to the 2003 and 2007 Women's World Cup titles. They continued to star for their national team as well as their respective club teams after those tournaments. However, a new generation of young German stars also emerged. Among them was midfielder Fatmire "Lira" Bajramaj. She has shown a knack for scoring goals. Even younger than Bajramaj is Alexandra Popp. In 2010, the striker led Germany to the Under-20 Women's World Cup title. She was named the tournament's best player. While not playing for Germany, Popp plays in the German women's professional league.

Sweden has long been a top national team as well. Midfielder Caroline Seger is poised to lead the next generation of Sweden teams. She is known for her great dribbling skills and for her toughness. Outside of her national team, Seger played for the WPS team Philadelphia

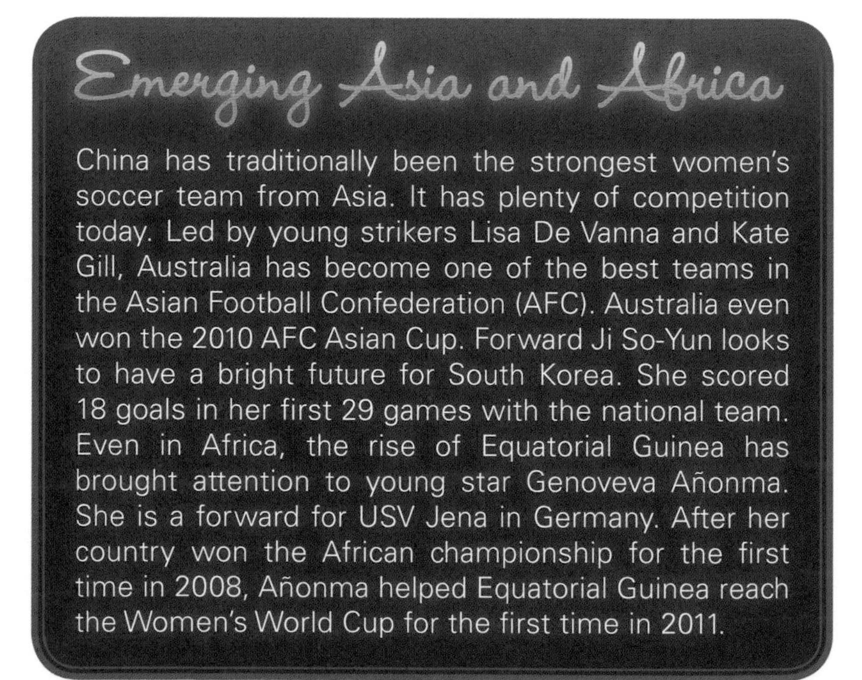

Emerging Asia and Africa

China has traditionally been the strongest women's soccer team from Asia. It has plenty of competition today. Led by young strikers Lisa De Vanna and Kate Gill, Australia has become one of the best teams in the Asian Football Confederation (AFC). Australia even won the 2010 AFC Asian Cup. Forward Ji So-Yun looks to have a bright future for South Korea. She scored 18 goals in her first 29 games with the national team. Even in Africa, the rise of Equatorial Guinea has brought attention to young star Genoveva Añonma. She is a forward for USV Jena in Germany. After her country won the African championship for the first time in 2008, Añonma helped Equatorial Guinea reach the Women's World Cup for the first time in 2011.

Independence in 2010 before being traded to the Western New York Flash in 2011. Swedish striker Lotta Schelin also emerged as a top goal-scorer while playing in the 2004 and 2008 Olympic Games as well as the 2007 Women's World Cup. She plays professionally in France.

Meanwhile, France's Sonia Bompastor has proven herself to be one of the most versatile players in the world. She made a name for herself in France as a great defender. She moved to the midfield when she joined the WPS Washington Freedom in 2009. She scored six goals and added 11 assists in two seasons in the WPS.

NEW U.S. STARS

As a four-year-old growing up in Rochester, New York, Abby Wambach scored so many goals during her first soccer season that she was transferred to a boys' team. She hasn't stopped scoring them. Wambach went on to star at the University of Florida, in the WUSA, WPS, and especially for the U.S. women's national team.

Wambach debuted for the national team in 2001. By 2002, she was combining with Mia Hamm to create a goal-scoring force on the WUSA's Washington Freedom as well as the national team. The two combined for 66 points during the Freedom's championship season in 2003.

Hamm helped Wambach become a top player for the national team as well. Wambach's extra-time goal at the

2004 Olympic Games ended Hamm's international career with a gold medal. The younger striker continued to thrive after her mentor retired. The hard-nosed Wambach became a leader for Team USA. At her second Women's World Cup in 2007, she scored six goals in six games as Team USA finished third. Two years later, she rejoined the Freedom when the team returned as part of WPS.

Wambach missed the 2008 Olympic Games due to an injury. But upon her recovery, she quickly regained her position as the leading forward for Team USA.

During the late 1990s, one might have guessed that Hope Solo would soon be leading the U.S. national team in scoring. After all, she scored 109 goals during her high school years in Washington. But it was after switching to goalkeeper in college that Solo truly made her mark.

Solo first played for the national team in 2000—one year after graduating high school. By 2005, she had overtaken longtime U.S. goalie Briana Scurry as the team's starter. However, the two were at the center of controversy at the 2007 Women's World Cup. Solo was the goalie as Team USA went unbeaten in its first four games. But in the semifinals, she was benched in favor of Scurry. The United States ended up losing to Brazil 4–0. Solo caused a controversy when she questioned the coach's decision to take her out. Many felt Solo should not have spoken to the press about an internal team matter.

▲ *Forward Abby Wambach (20) is one of the players Team USA is hoping can lead it back to another Women's World Cup title.*

The acrobatic goalie did not let the criticism bring her down, though. She was again the starting goalie as Team USA won the 2008 Olympic Games. Solo then went on to star for various teams in WPS.

Players like Marta, Prinz, Solo, and Wambach are leading a new generation of women's soccer stars on the top level. And with professional leagues around the world and college, high school, and youth teams around the country, the opportunities appear endless for women's soccer players.

GLOSSARY

confederation: A regional organization comprised of national soccer federations that organizes the sport in those areas. There are six confederations within FIFA.

draw: The result when a game is tied at the end of regulation. Soccer games end in a draw unless the game is in the knockout round of a tournament.

dynasty: A team that is very good over a long period of time.

extra time: Played only if the score is tied after regulation during an elimination game in a tournament, two 15-minute periods in which the teams continue play. If the game is still tied after that, the final result is determined by a shootout.

friendly: In soccer, referring to an exhibition game.

goal area: Within the penalty area, this extends six yards (5.5 m) out from the goal line. Goal kicks must be taken from within this space.

hat tricks: Games in which one player scores three goals.

header: When a player shoots or passes the ball by using her head. Proper heading technique involves using the forehead, not the top of the head, which can be dangerous to a player's health.

juke: Any move to get around a defender.

penalty area: The large box that extends 18 yards (16.5 m) out from the goal line and is 44 yards (40 m) wide. This is the only place the goalkeeper can use her hands.

penalty shootout: If an elimination game is still tied after regulation and extra time, a penalty shootout determines the winner. Each team has five players take penalty kicks. If the score is still tied after five kicks, they become sudden-death kicks.

points: Goals and assists.

red card: Given to a player for a harmful or dangerous foul, as well as for other unsportsmanlike conduct. A player who receives a red card is ejected and cannot be replaced.

referee: The official who enforces the rules during a soccer game. The referee roams the field while an assistant referee is stationed along each sideline.

scholarships: Money given to students to help them pay for classes or other college expenses as a reward for skills in specific areas, such as athletics.

stoppage time: Added to the end of each half to account for stoppages in play due to injuries and other breaks in play.

tactics: Strategy and game-planning that includes determining formations as well as how to attack and defend as a team.

technical skills: On-the-ball skills, including dribbling, passing, and shooting.

trap: Receive a pass by controlling the ball.

volleys: Shots or passes in which a player hits the ball with her foot while it is in midair.

yellow card: A caution given to a player for a reckless foul. Two yellow cards are equivalent to a red card.

FOR MORE INFORMATION

BOOKS

Akers, Michelle, and Tim Nash. *Standing Fast, Battles of a Champion*. Graham, NC: JTC Sports, Inc., 1997.
Co-Player of the Century Michelle Akers shares her inspiring story of triumph and courage through various injuries and other struggles in her playing career.

Hamm, Mia, and Aaron Heifetz. *Go for the Goal: A Champion's Guide to Winning in Soccer and Life.* New York: It Books, 2000.
Legend Mia Hamm talks about how she became the player that she did and gives tips on how to train and stay strong both mentally and physically.

Longman, Jere. *The Girls of Summer: The U.S. Women's Soccer Team and How It Changed the World.* New York: Harper, 2000.
This book is a firsthand account of the 1999 U.S. women's national team's journey to a Women's World Cup championship.

Lopez, Sue. *Women on the Ball: A Guide to Women's Soccer.* London, UK: Scarlet Press, 1997.
A guide to the history of women's soccer, with a focus on England.

WEBSITES

FIFA
www.FIFA.com
The official website of FIFA, the world governing body for soccer.

NCAA
www.ncaa.com
The official website of the National Collegiate Athletic Association, which governs college athletics.

U.S. Women's Soccer Team
www.ussoccer.com/Teams/US-Women.aspx
The official website for the U.S. women's national team includes news about the top U.S. players and the national team's games.

Women's Professional Soccer
www.womensprosoccer.com
The official website of Women's Professional Soccer, the top division of women's soccer in the United States and one of the best leagues in the world.

INDEX

PLACES TO VISIT

The Home Depot Center

18400 Avalon Boulevard, Carson CA 90746
www.homedepotcenter.com
(310) 630-2020
One of the first stadiums in the United States built specifically for soccer, the Home Depot Center frequently plays host to U.S. women's national team games and training sessions.

U.S. Olympic Training Center

One Olympic Plaza, Colorado Springs, CO 80909
www.teamusa.org
(888) 659-8687 or (719) 866-4618
The Olympic Training Center offers free public tours that include a video and a walking tour of the complex.

ABOUT THE AUTHOR

Jeff Kassouf began covering soccer at age 17. He is founder, owner, and operator of equalizersoccer.com, a WPS news site. He also writes WPS columns for SportsIllustrated.com and has won awards for his writing. Additionally, he does freelance soccer public relations writing and has collected two United Soccer Leagues Communications Awards.

ABOUT THE CONTENT CONSULTANT

Jack Huckel has been involved with soccer for almost 50 years in various ways. In 2000, he became the Director of Museum and Archives for the National Soccer Hall of Fame and Museum, researching, documenting, and presenting the history of the game to museum visitors. He continues to play soccer regularly and research the history of the game.